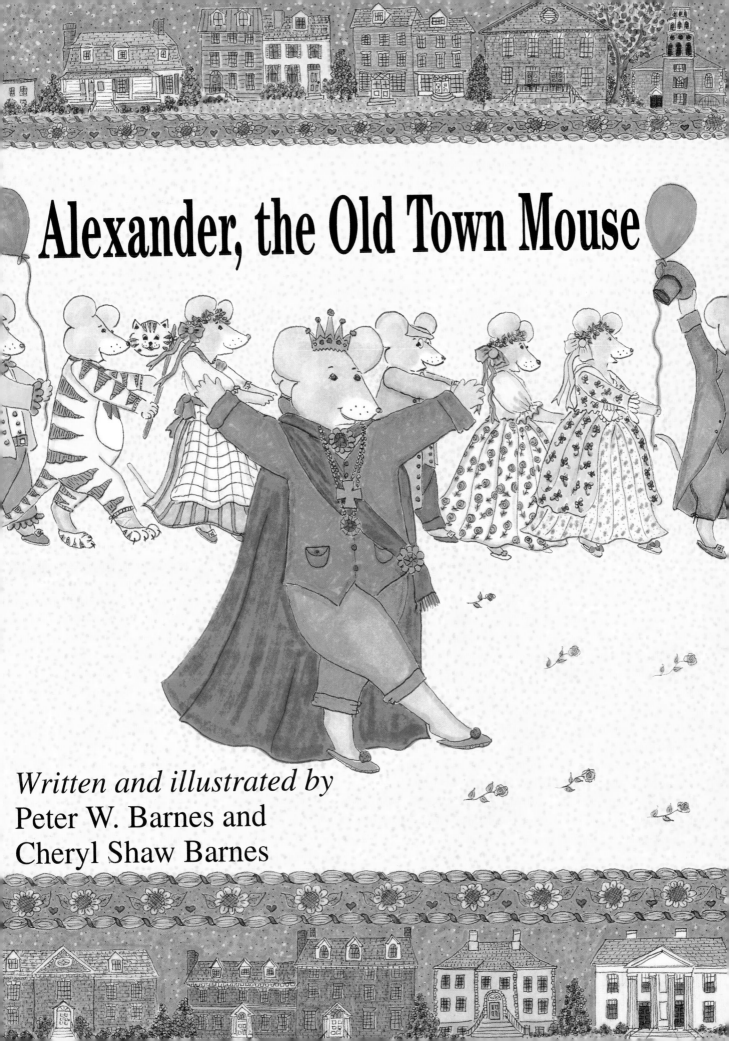

Alexander, the Old Town Mouse

Written and illustrated by
Peter W. Barnes and
Cheryl Shaw Barnes

Other VSP books by Peter and Cheryl Barnes

Woodrow, the White House Mouse, about the presidency and the nation's most famous mansion.

House Mouse, Senate Mouse, about Congress and the legislative process.

Marshall, the Courthouse Mouse, about the Supreme Court and the judicial process.

A "Mice" Way to Learn About Government teachers curriculum guide for the three books above.

Capital Cooking with Woodrow and Friends, a cookbook for kids that mixes fun recipes with fun facts about American history and government.

Woodrow For President, about voting, campaigns, elections and civic participation.

A "Mice" Way to Learn about Voting, Campaigns and Elections teachers curriculum guide for *Woodrow for President.*

Nat, Nat, the Nantucket Cat (with Susan Arciero), about beautiful Nantucket Island, Mass.

Martha's Vineyard (with Susan Arciero), about wonderful Martha's Vineyard, Mass.

Cornelius Vandermouse, the Pride of Newport (with Susan Arciero), about historic Newport, R.I., home to America's most magnificent mansion houses.

Also from VSP Books

Mosby, the Kennedy Center Cat, by Beppie Noyes, based on the true story of a wild stage cat that lived in the Kennedy Center in Washington D.C. (Autographed copies not available.)

Order these books through your local bookstore by title,
or order **autographed copies** of the Barnes' books by calling **1-800-441-1949**,
or from our website at **www.VSPBooks.com**.

For a brochure and ordering information, write to:

VSP Books
P.O. Box 17011
Alexandria, VA 22302

To get on the mailing list, send your name and address to the address above.

ISBN 0-9637688-1-6

10 9 8 7 6 5 4

Printed in the United States of America

This work is dedicated to my mother,
Shirley M. Shaw, a wonderful, loving Mom
and Nanna who has inspired all of us
to do good. You are the best in my book!
Thanks for everything.
—C.S.B.

ACKNOWLEDGMENTS

Love and thanks to my two beautiful girls, Maggie and Kate, for their
excitement and encouragement throughout this project—now I have no
more excuses not to take them shopping! Thanks to my father, Charles S.
Shaw, for always believing in me, and to Steve, Susan and the boys, and
Charlie, Martha and the kids—I have one terrific family! Thanks to
Denise Altholz, my best pal, for her friendship and support, and to her
husband, Walter, for his last minute poetic contributions. Love and thanks
to my hometown of Alexandria, the inspiration for this book. And special
thanks to my husband and partner, Peter, one tough editor—
you helped me realize my dreams!
—C.S.B.

Alexander M. (for Montgomery) Mouse
    Gazed into the fire that warmed his old house.
He thought to himself, as he rocked in his chair,
    "The Ball is tomorrow—I've got nothing to wear!"

"Cousin Emma may have a nice costume or two,
    With lots of bright colors—maybe red, green and blue
A robe and a crown and some jewels would be nice.
    Everyone will be dazzled! (At least all the mice.)"

The very next morning, Alexander M. Mouse
Ran down Alfred Street to the old Firehouse.
He jumped up each step on the creaky staircase,
Then went in the door to Mouse Emma Lee's place.

He declared, "Emma Lee, favorite cousin of mine,
   I must have a costume—something smart, something fine!
I want to look 'kingly' for the Mousquerade Ball.
   But as of right now, I have nothing at all."

"I can make you a robe," Emma said with a laugh,
  "If we take this red kerchief and fold it in half."
"It's okay," Alexander replied, with a frown,
  "But I just don't look kingly without jewels or a crown."

"Don't fret, Alexander," Cousin Emma Lee said.
"Cousin Will can help, too, if he's not still in bed.
For down in his basement, in Grandma's old trunk,
    You might find some jewelry mixed in with the junk."

Alexander M. (for Montgomery) Mouse,
    Knocked twice on the door of the old Ramsay House.
Cousin Will soon appeared, grey hair all a mess.
    "Wait here," he said, yawning, "until I get dressed."

They found jewels galore, and plenty of junk,
    As they rummaged around down in Grandma's old trunk.
And when Alexander reached all the way down,
    Right there at the bottom—a shiny, gold crown!

"Hooray, Cousin Will! Now my costume's complete!
  I look very 'kingly' from my head to my feet!
But now I must go, for it's getting quite late,
  For I told Cousin Emma we would meet her at eight!"

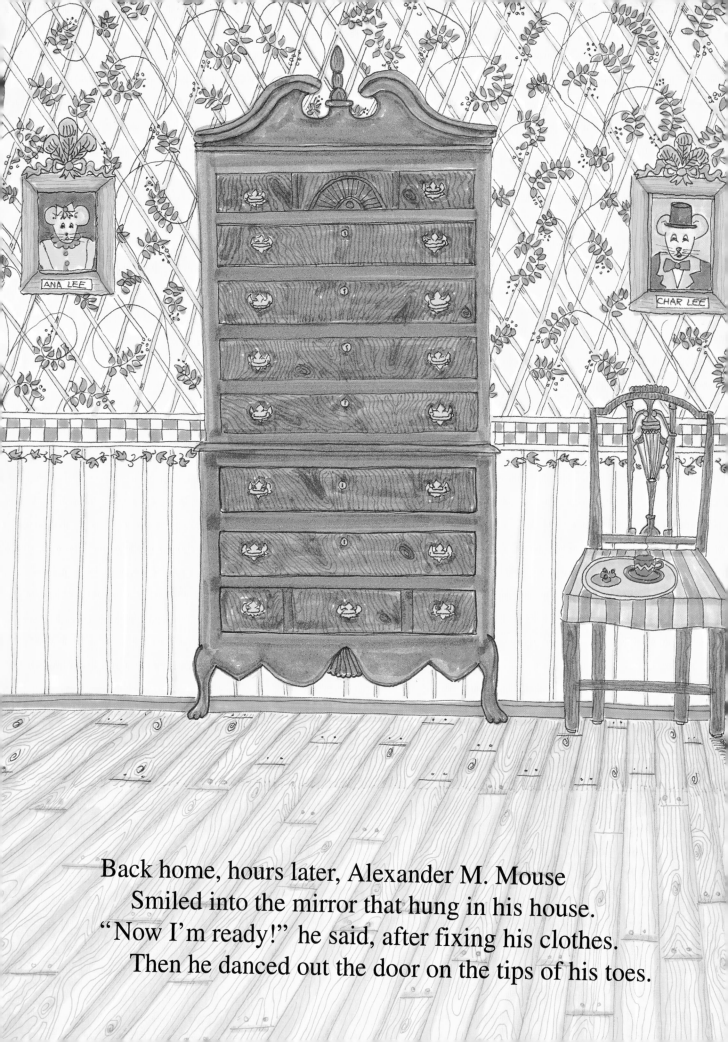

Back home, hours later, Alexander M. Mouse
   Smiled into the mirror that hung in his house.
"Now I'm ready!" he said, after fixing his clothes.
   Then he danced out the door on the tips of his toes.

Gadsby's Tavern was lit, a most festive display,
   Much the same as it looked in George Washington's day.
A feast in the Great Room, a dance in the Hall—
   What a glorious night for the Mousquerade Ball!

here were mouse Lords and Ladies, and mouse acrobats,
Mouse knights and mouse jesters—and even mouse cats!
here were ribbons and bows and balloons, if you please,
Mouse cookies and candies and lots of Swiss cheese!

Soon, the Mouster of Ceremonies said, "Gather near!
   It's time to announce 'Best Dressed Mouse of the Year'!
And the winner this time, for the best mouse disguise—
   Come on up, Alexander—you have won the Grand Prize!"

Every eye was upon him, every eye in the place!
    Alexander was shocked—you could tell from his face!
He heard the applause, got a kiss on the cheek.
    Then he jumped to the stage, and he started to squeak:

"Many thanks for this honor you've given to me.
But my thanks most of all to my mouse family!
To Will and to Emma—what more can I say!
Without you, I would not be a King for the Day!"

"Bravo!" they all shouted. "Hooray!" they yelled twice.
Then the music began for the Waltz of the Mice—
That's the way that the Mousquerade Ball always ends,
For Mouse Alexander and all his mouse friends.

He yawned as he walked down the cobblestone street.
   The Ball was great fun—now his day was complete.
He had done quite a lot—a big day for a mouse.
   Now it's home to his warm Alexandria house.

HISTORICAL NOTES

Alexandria, Virginia, was founded in 1749 by Scottish merchants on the Potomac River, across from Washington, D.C. The streets and boundaries were laid out by county surveyor John West; one of his assistants was young George Washington. The port city was a center of colonial trade. The waterfront wharves were the shipping point for tobacco and other crops grown on nearby Virginia farms and plantations.

Alexander's first stop, Friendship Firehouse, 107 South Alfred Street, was built for the Friendship Fire Company, which was established in 1774. The current firehouse was erected in 1855 and restored in 1992. Today, it is a museum and houses hand-drawn fire engines, axes, buckets and other historic fire fighting equipment.

Alexander's second stop, the Ramsay House, 221 King Street, was built around 1724 and was home to one of the founders of Alexandria, William Ramsay. Today, it is Alexandria's official visitors' center.

Alexander's third stop, Gadsby's Tavern, 134 North Royal Street, is two tavern buildings, one built in 1770 and another built in 1792. It is named after John Gadsby, an Englishman who operated the buildings from 1796 to 1808. It was a center of Alexandria social, entertainment and meeting activity. Today, it is a museum.

In the story, Alexander walks down cobblestone streets past the historic row homes that give Old Town its quaint charm. Many of the homes were constructed in the 1700's and housed the hardworking merchants, craftsmen and their families who built the city.

Many of the furniture pieces and wallpapers in the scenes are illustrated from actual historical design.